THE
PRINCESS
COLLECTION

Princess Cadance and The Spring Hearts garden

Written by G. M. Berrow

Little, Brown and Company
New York Boston

Little, Brown and Company

Hachette Book Group
1290 Avenue of the Americas, New York, NY 10104
Visit us at lb-kids.com

Little, Brown and Company is a division of Hachette Book
Group, Inc.
The Little, Brown name and logo are trademarks of Hachette Book
Group, Inc.

The publisher is not responsible for websites (or their content)
that are not owned by the publisher.

First Edition: May 2016

ISBN 978-0-316-38930-3

10 9 8 7 6 5 4 3 2 1

RRD-C

Printed in the United States of America

For Christina Lucine—
the girl who makes crystals
shine bright

Contents

HeartSong

The Crystal Heart glowed with a pulsating light. Its glittering facets reflected on the ground in a brilliant spray that reached across the pavement and onto the hooves of the ponies lined up around it. Princess Cadance's elegant face was illuminated by a subtle blue glow, casting her furrowed brow with a soft haze.

This Heartsong hadn't gone at all as she had hoped. Usually, the annual Hearts and

Hooves Day Heartsong garnered so many ponies in attendance that not everypony could fit in the main plaza! Ponies of all ages would spill out onto the shimmering side streets. They would bring apple crates to stand on, craning their necks for a glimpse of the ever-glowing Crystal Heart and the popular young royals conducting the songs. This year, however, a horrible case of the pony sniffles had swept across the kingdom. Most of the residents were at home, snuggled in their beds.

Princess Cadance knew that it was a major problem, for the Heartsong was actually a very important event. If the Crystal Heart didn't receive regular bursts of light and love from the ponies of the land, it might break again and the entire kingdom would be in grave danger.

The Frozen North was always looming. After the events leading up to baby Flurry Heart's "crystalling," when the Crystal Heart had actually broken apart, Princess Cadance wasn't taking any chances with its health. The incident had already made this winter more frigid and blustery than the Empire was accustomed to, and the grounds had seen better days. It was imperative that the Crystal Heart be pumped full of love at all times. Otherwise, the entire Crystal Empire could be lost to the icy avalanches.

Cadance took a few steps toward the sparse crowd of Crystal Empire citizens. She shot a private, nervous look at her husband, Prince Shining Armor. The striking stallion replied with his signature encouraging nod. His blue mane fell over his eyes. *You can do it*, he assured her without even speaking. Princess Cadance nodded back. She felt braver now. Shining Armor always had that effect on her.

"Dearest Crystal ponies!" Cadance addressed the small crowd. "Each Hearts and Hooves Day, we join together so our love will warm us through the few remaining days of our frosty winter and carry us into our beautiful spring." Cadance pointed daintily at the Crystal Heart. Her candy-colored mane gently swayed in the winter wind.

"I thank you for sharing your voices and hearts with your fellow ponies on this special day!" The princess mustered a sunny smile. "Your kindness and love for one another rings true through each note and melody. I deliver my warm wishes to you and all your loved ones at home with the pony sniffles."

"And now, one last song!" called Shining Armor, cheery-faced and rose-cheeked, as he trotted forward. The royal baby, Princess Flurry Heart, rode on her father's back. She bounced along with her oversized wings outstretched, and giggled at each bumpy hoofstep. The crowd cooed. Shining Armor laughed as he addressed the citizens. "It's Flurry Heart's favorite!" Cadance signaled to the Crystal Sym-pony Orchestra, and a rich tune began to fill the air around them. The distinct opening notes of the Crystal flugelhorn trumpeted. Flurry squealed happily.

When the Crystal snow gets icy and chilly,
Join voices with every colt and every filly!
There's only one solution,
And we've made a resolution.

 5

We'll lift our spirits to the sky,
Our hearts grow full and our hooves rise
up high.
Hooves cold, hearts warm; cold hooves,
warm hearts!
Hearts and Hooves Day, we all take part.

Despite the small group, the voices grew strong as the song hit the crescendo. On the highest note, multiple bright bursts of light shot straight toward the Crystal Heart! A warm, happy feeling washed over everypony's glittering, crystalline face. As Princess Cadance scanned the contented kingdom, she knew that everything was going to be all right. Maybe it didn't matter after all that most of the ponies were at home, slurping get-well soup. The love in the Crystal

Empire was safe for another season. As the song came to an end, Cadance looked out at the shimmering buildings built with sturdy crystal and reminded herself that their home was stronger than it appeared.

"This Hearts and Hooves Day was just as awesome as the rest." Shining Armor lifted Flurry Heart from his back and placed her gently in the foal stroller. "See, Mi Amore?"

"You know I don't like to be called that name." Cadance frowned in a mocking way and nudged the stallion. She leaned down and tucked a soft blanket around Flurry Heart. The baby smiled, her big eyes blinking.

"I know—that's why I do it," he replied with a satisfied laugh. "But honestly, Cadance, don't you agree that maybe you were worrying

 7

a little too much about the Heartsong? It all turned out perfectly."

"I suppose you're right," Cadance admitted. "Still, I just hope everypony gets better soon."

"So do I," Shining Armor agreed, motioning toward the castle. "Now, let's go home and have a nice, quiet evening *inside*, where it's toasty? My flank is freezing out here!" Shining Armor could be sort of a colt when it came to chilly weather. Winter was his least favorite season, so naturally he liked to remind everypony of that all the time— another reason why Cadance couldn't wait until the bright sunshine of spring melted the snow and ice away. She shook her head, mildly amused at her husband shivering dramatically in an attempt to garner sympathy.

"Let's go warm you up, you funny little

colt," Cadance teased as she took one last glance at the Crystal Heart. Flurry Heart pointed her tiny hoof at it and gurgled. "What is it, sweetie?"

A group of five ponies who had been gathering near the gem waited patiently nearby. They hung back, pretending to inspect the facets up close, but the princess could read body language well enough to know that they were waiting to say hello to her. A teenaged Unicorn filly with a pink mane and a grumpy expression on her face caught Cadance's eye. The mint-green pony was shuffling her hooves around and looking off into the distance. There was something familiar about her, but Cadance couldn't quite put her hoof on it.

"Actually, you take Flurry Heart and

go ahead. Get the fire started," Cadance instructed her husband as she kept her eyes on the curious group. "I'll be along shortly to make you two some hot cocoa. I just need to take care of something first."

"Cocoa with marshmallows?" Shining Armor's face lit up with a giant smile, and he galloped off toward the castle. "My wife is the best!"

Princess Cadance laughed as she trotted back to the Crystal Heart. She had taken only a few steps before the group of ponies launched themselves right in front of her.

"Your Majesty!" exclaimed the self-elected leader of the group, a tall lavender mare with a cutie mark of a bunch of Crystal berries. She had her golden mane in the traditional updo of the region, with sparkling purple bands across her head. Once the mare opened her mouth, the words came rushing out.

"It is so lovely to see you, and may I say what a beautiful Heartsong that was? I haven't seen such a small turnout since I was a filly during the year that almost everypony traveled to the big Hearts and Hooves event in Canterlot. My mother wouldn't let me go. I don't even think I had my cutie mark yet! Wow, time flies, doesn't it? It feels as if it's been a thousand years—well, technically it has been, I suppose. Ha-ha! Get it? Because of King Sombra? Oh, listen to me rambling again!" The mare laughed. A young green filly rolled her eyes and followed it with a heavy sigh. The purple mare didn't notice or chose to ignore it. "Anyhow,

I don't know if you remember me, but I'm—"

"Lilac Quartz?" Cadance finished for her. As soon as the mare had begun talking, Cadance recognized her, which was a relief because the princess prided herself on trying to recall the names of everypony she met. "Of course I remember you. You run the Crystal Crown Café!" Memories of many delicious meals at the charming spot suddenly made her very hungry. "Do you still make that delectable carrot-ginger soup? It was my favorite thing to eat when I first arrived in the Crystal Empire."

Lilac Quartz blushed. The chatty mare was speechless!

"Yes, they do," chimed in one of her friends, Rose Water, with a massive grin. "You and the prince should *definitely* stop by sometime soon." Something about the delivery of her comment made Cadance think that the mare cared more about Shining Armor's presence

"*I* shall," Princess Cadance replied warmly with a little bow of her head. "And I can't wait to see that little filly of yours again, Lilac. She was so adorable, always covered in flour from baking Crystal berry tarts. How is she?"

"Your Majesty, you can ask my Olivine Jewel herself." Lilac Quartz smiled as she pointed her hoof at the moody young filly. "She's right there."

"My stars!" Cadance breathed in awe. "She's all grown up." Olivine Jewel was now staring at the Crystal Heart and frowning. She paced impatiently, clopping her hooves on the ground.

"Oh dearie," Lilac Quartz tutted, leaning in closer to Cadance to whisper. "Between you and me, Princess, she's not the same little filly she used to be. All doom and gloom with her these days, I'm afraid. Everything is either boring or embarrassing. Teenagers, you know? Wish I could find something to pique her interest!" Lilac's friends all shook their heads in support.

"Still no cutie mark…" commented Sweet Leaf.

Rose Water sighed. "And Olivine doesn't even like coming into the Crystal Crown Café anymore."

"I'm sure it's just a phase…." Cadance made a sympathetic face. She wasn't sure what to say to make the exhausted mother feel any better. It was true that Cadance herself used to be an expert on foal-sitting, but becoming a mother to Flurry Heart had been an entirely different endeavor. It was exhausting and confusing, but also the most wonderful experience that the princess could recall in her whole life. Cadance's heartstrings were wrapped tightly around her little foal. No doubt Lilac Quartz felt the same about her Olivine.

"Well, isn't *that* interesting!" Olivine shouted not two seconds later. She perked up, eyes bright, but remained focused on the Crystal Heart. "Mama, hurry over!"

"What is it, Olive?" Lilac Quartz brightened and trotted over, her three friends in tow. The mares crowded Cadance's view, but several shrieks suddenly escaped from the group. When the mares parted and

Cadance saw what they were looking at, she almost shrieked as well.

The soft blue light of the special gemstone was beating very slowly, almost coming to a complete stop. The Crystal Heart was dying!

Matters of the Crystal Heart

Princess Cadance burst into her living quarters, adrenaline coursing through her body as she scanned the cavernous space for her husband and foal. Cadance couldn't believe that her worst fears about today had come true after all. She was lucky that she'd stayed behind to talk with the group of mares and fillies. Otherwise she wouldn't have seen the dying Crystal Heart in time. Cadance had managed to boost the energy of the Heart with her powerful Alicorn magic, but it wouldn't last forever. She needed another plan.

Cadance, filled with dread, cantered through the halls of the castle.

The Crystal Heart was in terrible danger, and if Princess Cadance didn't fix it soon, the Crystal Empire would be, too. All she'd wanted was to see the ponies of her land filled with light and love and to watch the kingdom blossom into a beautiful spring—bees buzzing, pretty flowers blooming, and ponies prancing around and playing together. If the Heart stopped glowing and broke apart once more, there would never be spring again. The entire expanse and everypony in it would be covered with much worse than the normal winter—it would be an avalanche of snow from the Frozen North!

"Shining Armor!" the princess cried out as she galloped toward the couple's sitting room, where the fireplace was. "We have a problem! The Crystal Hea—*whoaaaaa*!" As if in slow motion, Cadance lost her hoofing. As she fell to the ground, she managed to glimpse the culprit responsible for her ungraceful tumble. It was one of her gowns from a past gala. She'd tried it on earlier to see if she wanted to send it to Rarity for alterations and had carelessly tossed it onto the floor.

The moment Cadance hit the floor, she expected to hear a loud *thud*. But the impact made no sound at all because the princess had landed on a patch of grass.

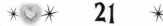

She looked up to see that she was now in a soft green garden with the sun shining on her pink face. The fresh air held the heavy, pleasant scent of flower blossoms. In the distance, intricate topiaries lined the horizon. Hundreds of ponies were laughing and singing. Where was she? A searing flash of blue momentarily blinded her, and she was back in the sitting room with her hoof tangled up in a gown.

"Cadance! What are you doing on the floor?" Shining Armor bolted over to help his wife, ditching the pile of logs he'd assembled. "Are you hurt?" Shining reached out his hoof.

"No, no. I'm all right…but I *am* confused," Cadance mused, trying to work out what exactly she had just seen. Had it been a dream? A premonition? Or had it just been her most sincere wish that had materialized to tease her? A beautiful spring day in the Crystal Empire garden...

"Confused?" Shining Armor asked with a sly smirk, picking up the dress from the floor and holding it up as evidence. "About why you are the most beautiful, prim-and-proper princess, but also secretly the *messiest* mare in all of the Crystal Empire?" He chuckled lovingly. He had not known that side of Cadance until they were married. Shining Armor's belongings—his precious comic books and games—were displayed neatly on his shelves, whereas Cadance's things were everywhere! The princess had many admirable qualities, but tidiness was not one of them.

When Cadance didn't giggle at his jab as she usually did, Shining Armor knew something was off. "What is it, Cady? You look kind of strange. *Kind of* like you just had—"

"One of my visions." Cadance confirmed, her almond-shaped eyes widening as she met his. She nodded in disbelief. "I can't figure it out. It's been years since I've had any that strong, and now *two* in one day!"

Ever since she was a little Pegasus filly, Cadance had received hazy visions of the future. They were random and uncontrollable, but they almost always were fulfilled. After many years of observing the unique magical ability as she watched Cadance grow, Princess Celestia believed the talent had come to Cadance through Prismia, the evil enchantress Cadance had defeated as a young pony. Not many ponies knew of this gift. Of course, Shining Armor was one of the few who did. Princess Cadance could keep nothing from her best friend.

"Whoa, two visions?" Shining Armor cocked his head.

"This morning, before the Heartsong, I saw another. It was why I was so worried about everypony being too sick to join in," she admitted. She let out a heavy sigh and trotted over to her favorite cushy chair, hoping to find some respite. "I saw the Crystal Heart. The light went completely out of it, just like when Sombra ruled." She shuddered thinking about the fight against the evil tyrant stallion who once enslaved the Crystal ponies under his wretched rule.

"Aw, Cadance. I *know* it's taken a long time for the Crystal ponies to recover from that nasty dude, but we're safe now." He patted her hoof. Shining Armor was such an optimist sometimes. "We should do our best to forget about him."

"I love your positivity, Shiny dearest," Cadance replied with candor. "But I disagree. Even if King Sombra never returns, we still must look to the Crystal Heart to protect us." Cadance stood up, determined. "And I'm going to make sure it happens. It's my duty as reigning princess of this land— *our* duty—to be absolutely sure everypony is safe not only today, but always!"

"Well, I can't argue with my clever wife on *that*," Shining Armor admitted. "But how are we going to do it?"

"By fulfilling my other vision, of course." Cadance smiled, thinking of the old garden on the outskirts of the castle grounds. She'd never actually visited it, but she had heard ponies speak about the area from time to time.

"The Crystal Empire is clearly destined to have an amazing celebration in the garden, and I'm going to make it happen. The ponies are going to be filled with so much love and light that we'll never have to worry again!" Cadance rose and did a little victory twirl. Her violet, rose, and gold mane billowed out like a flouncy skirt.

"Cool with me." Shining Armor shrugged with a smile. "But can we at least have that hot cocoa first?"

CHAPTER

3

Castle Grounded

The morning felt much warmer than the previous one. Princess Cadance took it as a good indication that winter would be fully wrapped up soon—perfect timing to execute her brilliant idea. As she trotted across the castle grounds to go inspect the venue with a sleepy Shining Armor in tow, Cadance began to brainstorm all the ways to make this Heartsong do-over a success. Along with fragrant flowers and sunshine, there would have to be topiaries, of course—she'd seen that much in her vision. The rest of the details were open to improvisation. They could hold a parade, with floats decorated entirely with fresh flowers! And perhaps she'd commission the bakers to make a violet cream cake....

"Hurry up, Shining Armor," Cadance urged. "We have so much to do!"

The couple wasn't even halfway to the garden before they were interrupted. A beefy stallion from the Royal Guard galloped over, looking precise and perfect as ever. He was out of breath. "Your Majesties," he said with a bow, "I do beg your pardon... but I have...an important scroll...from Princess Celestia."

"It's no problem at all." Cadance returned

his bow. "Thank you for your promptness in delivering it. Where is the scroll?"

"Apologies, Princess," the guard said, blushing, "but the scroll is meant for Commander Shining Armor's eyes only. Royal Guard business. Strict instructions."

The prince, who was still a bit bleary-eyed, straightened as if he were under inspection by an invisible chief commander. "Really?" He used the magic from his Unicorn horn to unfurl it and quickly scanned the contents. Whatever it was, his expression was quite serious.

"Bad news?" Cadance pried, leaning in her pink muzzle to sneak a peek. But Shining Armor rolled it back up quickly before she was able to make out anything on the page.

Shining Armor smoothed down his messy blue mane. "It's just pretty much that I've been told to hold our new Royal Guard recruitment trials early. Celestia wants me to start right away."

"What a strange request...." Cadance tilted her head, causing her golden crown to glint in the morning sunlight. "Did she say why?" The princesses didn't normally keep things from one another. Not unless there was a good reason.

"No, she just explained that it was 'important' to take precautions." Shining Armor pulled Cadance into a hug. "But I've got it all taken care of, so *don't worry*." He leaned in and touched his horn to Cadance's, nuzzling her face. He lowered his voice to a whisper. "Please get somepony to help you with all this. I know how you like to do everything yourself, but I don't want you to wear yourself out...."

"You worry far too much," Princess Cadance said with a smile and a wink. "I'm perfectly capable. Besides, it'll be really simple! Just a few decorations and we'll be ready for spring."

"Okay..." Shining Armor lifted a brow. "But just leave the training fields alone?"

"Nope, I'm decorating those, too!" she teased as she waved at Shining Armor and his guard. Then Cadance set off to finish the task at hoof, feeling more excited with each trot. This was going to be so much fun, and the perfect way to power the Crystal Heart.

A crumbling signpost in the near distance guided the way. It read: EMPIRE GARDEN, BY MASTER GARDENER "A. S." Cadance followed the arrow and came upon a set of partially shattered crystal gates. As she gingerly pushed them open and pranced inside, the pink princess gasped at her surroundings, utterly speechless because of what she saw. It certainly was a sight to behold, but not the nice one she'd expected. Instead of a well-manicured place to frolic and play, the garden was nothing but a dilapidated mess.

CHAPTER
4

A Growing Idea

"How in Equestria did this happen?" Cadance wondered as she began to explore the withered area. Everywhere the princess looked, there were rows upon rows of overgrown hedges, dead flowers, and piles of dirt. Instead of the golden pots meant to contain the topiaries shaped like animals, all Cadance found were some large ceramic vessels with broken, peeling tree stems lining the stone pathways like sad soldiers.

As she wandered, Cadance wondered if she had read it all wrong. Perhaps her blurry vision was supposed to be taking place in a different area of the grounds. Or maybe it was not her destiny at all. It was quite possible that the sad, old garden was just what it appeared to be—hopeless and broken beyond repair. But on the other hoof, with some extra love it *could* be blossoming in no time. Cadance smiled, coming to a realization. Love was always the answer.

The princess closed her violet eyes and inhaled. The air was still fresh and the sun was still shining on her face. That was plenty to get started!

A few hours into working on cleaning up the garden, a couple of things were becoming clear to the princess: She didn't know very much about landscaping or gardening, and this project was going to be a much bigger task than she'd anticipated. Even with the aid of her strong magic to help her lift, move, and dig things, she was still just one pony. Cadance was going to need some helping hooves. *Fast.*

A murmur of voices nearby disrupted Cadance's quiet moment. Across the massive expanse of grass, a large group of young teenage fillies and colts followed a castle tour guide. An older mare with a red mane led the way. She was chatting and calling out to the group. The young ponies hardly paid attention because they were too busy whispering with their friends or daydreaming.

It reminded Cadance of her days living back in Canterlot with Princess Celestia and Princess Luna. Sometimes Cadance helped out by giving tours around the castle to school groups. The young ponies would always drag their hooves in boredom through the whole thing until the very end of the day—when they got to help cook a meal for their class in the castle kitchens. The ponies would suddenly become engaged and playful when they had a way to contribute.

Princess Cadance left the garden and headed straight for the tour group with a seed of an idea growing in her head. She needed extra hooves, and they needed something to occupy themselves with.

"Welcome to the castle!" Princess Cadance called out. Everypony turned to look at her, quite surprised to find the princess covered in soil and wandering around by herself. "Pardon my appearance," Cadance laughed, trotting up closer to them, "but I've just been working on a little project down at the garden, and I heard voices."

"Your Majesty!" the tour guide mare gasped, and bowed. "I was just taking this school group around to the back entrance. If I'd known you were here, we could have taken a different route—"

"Don't be silly, Petal Shine," replied Cadance, picking a leaf out of her mane. "I'm actually extremely glad to see all of you!" She scanned the faces of the young ponies. They all looked a little starstruck except for... Olivine Jewel. The green filly stood at the back of the group on her own, wearing her permanent grumpy expression. Cadance smiled at her. "Hello, Olivine!"

At this, Olivine's entire class and teacher spun around to look at the young filly, shocked. A blush appeared on her cheeks as the ponies began to whisper to one another. How was Olivine on a first-name basis with the princess?

"It is so lovely to meet you, Your Majesty. I'm Ruby Jubilee!" The teacher stepped up to Cadance, shivering with enthusiasm. "And this is my class. We're exploring careers at the castle today! Do you have any tips for our little ponies here?"

"Just follow your hearts," offered Cadance warmly. "It always leads to the right decision, if you listen."

"Splendid advice. Thank you, Princess!"

Ruby Jubilee cooed. "Hear that, class? Princess Cadance—"

"But what about following your cutie mark?" a stocky blue colt with a shaggy mane called out. "Isn't that what we're supposed to do?" His cutie mark was a picture of a mop.

Olivine began to shuffle her hooves. She kicked a clump of dirt.

"Yeah! That is what we're supposed to do," called out a yellow filly with a muffin cutie mark. A few other ponies nodded in agreement. Ruby Jubilee shot them all a stern teacher look. "Mop Top, Citrine— let's not bother the princess with too many questions."

"Oh, I don't mind!" Cadance knew to choose her words carefully. "Your cutie marks are definitely important, but some very special fillies in Ponyville recently helped remind me that a cutie mark is just one part of you. Everypony can be wonderful at all sorts of things. You just have to try!" Cadance procured a scroll from her saddlebag and unfurled it. It was a rough map of the garden. "For example, how would you all like to try something new with me? I'm planning a big garden celebration in honor of spring, and I would love for you to come join me."

The teacher's jaw dropped. "You want *my* Crystal Preparatory students to help you with your special project?" Ruby Jubilee squealed with delight. "Wow! Why, of course they would love to! It would be such an honor!" Another wave of whispers broke out among the students, but this time they sounded like excited ones.

"That's wonderful news!" Cadance sighed in relief. "Now all we need is to tell the rest of the kingdom."

"And do *all* the work," muttered Olivine. "*Or* you could just hire a professional gardener pony."

But nopony listened to her, as usual.

CHAPTER

5

Helping Hooves

By the time Princess Cadance made it down to the garden the next morning, the young ponies had been up for hours and work was in full swing. Cadance's heart felt full as she watched the progress that had been made by the hooves of Crystal Empire citizens. They had already begun repainting the pots a shimmering gold color, digging up weeds, and replenishing the soil to make way for brand-new foliage.

The teacher, Ruby Jubilee, marched around with the scroll in her hoof trying to match Cadance's plans to the tasks everypony was assigned. Mop Top and Citrine were currently working together to weave rainbow ribbons and white lights into the roof of the old gazebo. Below the pair, a pink Unicorn named Gemma and a golden Earth pony called Sweet Éclair were coating the gazebo with white paint. The two ponies whistled happily as they wielded their brushes, laughing every so often when one of them accidentally splashed paint onto the other.

Even though the work was tough, the ponies seemed happy to be doing something important. Princess Cadance grabbed a shovel and started helping out. She felt lucky to have stumbled upon such a lovely group of ponies. She was having so much fun, too!

When some castle attendants came down to fetch the princess for some important state business, Cadance didn't want to go. She felt terrible about leaving her new helpers, but Ruby Jubilee insisted that her class would be just fine carrying on without her for now. *Duty calls*, Cadance thought, vowing to come back as soon as possible.

Over by a row of flower beds, Olivine frowned and shook her head as she watched the royal trot back toward the castle. "She's *leaving*? Who does she think she is?"

"Duh, Olive, a *princess*," said an orange mare named Fire Opal as she plopped another giant Funflower into the soil. Her rainbow-striped mane had pieces of dirt and leaves sticking out of it. "She has tons of other work to do instead of gardening. Besides, I bet it's all boring meetings and stuff. She probably wants to stay here with us because it's so awesome!"

"It's very enjoyable," agreed Star Seed. The purple Unicorn with a wavy blue mane closed her eyes, smiling. "I'm feeling so in tune with nature.... It's making me really relaxed." Star Seed stifled a big yawn.

"No, Star," Olivine sassed back. "You're tired because we're all being *forced* to do community service for the castle! It's so unfair."

"Olive, why do you always have to be such a grump? We're *not* being forced. We want to help Princess Cadance with the garden," replied Fire Opal, a hint of annoyance in her voice. "The celebration is going to be the best ever. Did you hear we are going to have a parade where all the floats are covered completely with flowers?"

"Really?" Star Seed perked up. "That's so cool. I'm definitely vibing on that." She closed her eyes again and sat down on the grass. "I'm digging this, too."

"Plus," Fire Opal continued, "Princess Cadance said we could use 'artistic license' and plant whatever flowers we want. I think it's really neat of her to let us design stuff for the castle. It's good experience."

"I have an idea. Let's try to make our sections of the garden really unique...." Star Seed said dreamily as she looked up at the clouds. "Like, pretty and weird at the same time, you know?"

"I love that!" Fire Opal chirped. "Then the ponies who want something a little different can come to our spot."

"Whatever. I hate this garden." Olivine kicked a shovel with her hoof. "It's no use trying to fix it anyway. It's never going to be like it was before King Sombra."

"Yeah, right." Fire Opal rolled her eyes. "Like *you* actually remember what it was like before King Sombra."

"Yes, I do!" Olivine stood up, growing annoyed. Her pink mane frizzed out around her face, making her look a little frantic. "And if we actually tried to re-create it…the garden would look way better than this mess. I…I…can show you how it used to look to prove it!"

"How?" Fire Opal and Star Seed exchanged an unconvinced look. It was well known that Olivine was always throwing fits over the tiniest things and making up stories for attention. It was probably because she didn't have her cutie mark yet, but it's not as if anypony ever teased her about that. The real reason why nopony liked to hang out with Olivine was because she was so moody.

"Just come with me and I'll show you," Olivine said, sincere and calm for once. "Please?"

CHAPTER 6

The greenhouse

The crumbling cottage was all the way on the outskirts of the city, tucked away near a shimmering Crystal lake. It was chillier than the center of the Empire, so there was still a light frost covering every surface. Olivine had yet to reveal to Fire Opal and Star Seed whom they were going to visit. They just knew that the pony in question was very mysterious. The three ponies crouched in the Crystal berry bushes near the front door.

"So who lives here?" Fire Opal whispered. "Can you tell us now?" Her eyes were alight with intrigue. "A zebra who can concoct potions? A bat-pony? Daring Do?"

"My grandpa," Olivine said reverently, a sparkle in her eye. She crouched low as she trotted to the front door, signaling for the others to follow her. "Come on!"

"Your *what*?" Fire Opal stood up, no longer caring about keeping quiet. She turned to Star Seed. "Is she joking right now? Did she bring us all this way to visit her Guh-*randpa*?"

Star Seed shrugged in response and smiled, popping a Crystal berry into her mouth. Not much fazed her.

But they'd come this far. The two ponies had no choice but to follow Olive through the door.

"*Shhh!*" Olive hissed when it slammed closed behind Star Seed. "We can't wake him." She gestured to an old stallion, snoozing peacefully in a big velvet chair. His glasses were one snore away from falling off his muzzle, and his white mane frizzed out in every direction, just like Olivine's.

"I just need to find one thing from here," whispered Olive, tip-hoofing through the room. "Don't touch anything!"

The old house was packed with shelves upon shelves of well-loved, dusty books and hundreds of potted plants of every variety. The combination of the warm temperature and the sunlight streaming in through the skylight made it feel like a cozy greenhouse. Star Seed, who seemed to like it, started looking through one of the bookshelves.

As the Unicorn scanned the titles, she began to notice a theme. Almost all the books were about plants, seeds, or spells! She ran her hoof gently along the spines and picked one that was displayed prominently, entitled *Indigenous Magical Plants of the North and South, Volume 5: Flowers.* She was reading about a flower called a Lazilily, which supposedly filled ponies with lethargy, when somepony called her name. Star Seed put the book down on the table and quickly trotted to join the others outside. Olivine and Fire Opal were staring at a small wooden box full of tiny pouches.

Fire Opal crinkled her nose. "What are they?"

"Supposedly, they're magical seeds," Olivine explained with a grin. She picked up a blue pouch and poured a few shimmering specks out onto her hoof. "My grandpa Alabaster has been collecting them forever. He always said that if planted, they would grow into the prettiest and *weirdest* flowers ever."

"I like the sound of that," Star Seed said, nodding in approval. "But *how* weird?"

"And what makes them magical?" Fire Opal raised a suspicious eyebrow. For the first time ever, there was a flicker of real excitement in Olivine's eyes.

"I don't know. But we're going to plant them in the castle garden and find out."

CHAPTER 7

Float On

The air outside was warm enough for the doors leading to the balcony in Cadance and Shining Armor's castle bedroom to be kept open. A gentle breeze floated through the space as the princess readied for dinner. Cadance hummed a tune to herself while brushing her long, soft mane into its pretty curls. She placed her golden crown atop her head. It had felt like ages since she and her husband had been able to carve out the time to sit down together for a real meal. And now that Flurry Heart was old enough to stay with the castle foal-sitter, the young royals could finally have a moment for each other. It would be so relaxing and well earned.

"May I escort the lovely mare to the dining room?" Shining Armor appeared at the doorway wearing a white waistcoat and a cheesy grin on his face. He nodded in a formal bow so low that his blue mane nearly touched the floor.

"You may." Cadance stifled a giggle and bowed back. "But please make it quick, because the lovely mare is starving!" Shining Armor laughed and held his hoof out to his wife. Cadance seemed to be in better spirits than ever, so he was happy.

When they got to the main castle dining

room, two places at the end of the banquet table were already set. A butler pony was waiting with a bottle of fresh apple cider. He motioned to the setup with a flourish and began to pour them each a glass.

"I feel relieved to see you smiling," admitted Shining Armor once they'd sat down at the massive table. "Sorry I've been so busy with the Royal Guard recruitment trials lately. It's just really important that we have a strong team, especially this year."

"I understand," assured Cadance. She still wondered what was in the contents of the letter from Princess Celestia, though. Needing more security for the Crystal Empire could mean that there was a potential threat. "But is everything okay?"

"Of course! How is the garden coming along?" Shining Armor queried, his mouth full of salad. "Are your student helpers having fun out there? Sure seems like it! I just saw three little ponies still digging around on my way here. Isn't it getting a bit late?"

"I know. Those little ponies have been so dedicated. Every time I go to the garden, they are planting more gorgeous, exotic flowers. I'm not sure how they are getting them to grow so fast, but it's amazing." Cadance scrunched up her nose. "I wanted to watch and learn their green-hoof secrets, but for some reason they don't want any extra help from me."

"They probably know you've got your hooves full as it is, sweetie."

"Well, they *are* right about that," Cadance admitted as she took a sip of cider. "There's still so much else to do to prepare. Besides the new garden, there's the maypole, the parade, the Heartsong music…"

Shining Armor's eyes grew wide. "Whoa there, filly! A parade, too?" His wife had the tendency to get carried away and put far too much on her plate when she got excited.

"A parade will only help spread the love throughout the entire Crystal Empire," the princess said, matter-of-fact. "Ponies have already been visiting the garden to collect flowers to use on their entries for the floral float competition." Cadance's almond-shaped eyes sparkled with delight. "You should see some of the designs! They are so beautiful and bright. Just what everypony needs to lift their spirits."

"That's awesome, Cady," commended Shining Armor. His face showed concern.

 65

"But do you think it will boost the Crystal Heart like you were hoping?"

Princess Cadance beamed. She had saved the best news for last.

"It already has."

"This isn't really what I pictured when you said the Crystal Heart got a boost...." Shining Armor craned his neck and gawked at the elaborate float. The structure looked like a giant version of the Crystal Heart, except this one was half covered with bluebells, delphiniums, and hydrangeas. A group of ponies was busy attaching even more blooms as the royals watched.

"I know." Princess Cadance motioned

with her pink hoof. "But don't the ponies look happy?"

Shining Armor nodded. He couldn't deny what he saw. "Totally!"

"Well, that's what's helping the Heart." Cadance trotted away and Shining Armor followed. She cantered past several other floats shaped like everything from giant flowers to Crystal berry cupcakes. Everything was covered in fragrant, fresh flowers. They smelled heavenly.

"Come look!"

Shining Armor and Cadance approached the real Crystal Heart around the corner. It was suspended between the two crystal spikes below the castle, as usual. But the strength was visibly steadier, glowing bright blue and flickering only every couple of minutes.

"It's still not enough, but I haven't had to use my magic to boost it again," Cadance explained. "The Garden Hearts Celebration is going to fix everything for good. I just *know* it."

"Your Majesty!" cried an aqua-colored mare, galloping up to the couple. Her face read distress. "I'm so glad you're here. We have an emergency—it's Petal Shine!"

"What is it, Emerald Gem?" Cadance snapped into alert mode. "Is she hurt?"

"Not exactly, but I think you should come look for yourself...."

The purple pony was lying on the ground, holding her stomach. At first, Petal Shine appeared to be shivering. But upon closer inspection, it became clear that the pony was just in a fit of uncontrollable giggles. "Can't...stop...hee-hee! Ha-ha!"

Petal Shine squirmed and wiggled. "Oh my! Ha-ha-ha!"

"What's so funny, Petal Shine?" Cadance was stumped. She hadn't heard a joke that hilarious in ages. Watching Petal Shine laugh so hard made her giggle herself. "Please share it with us!"

"No, Princess." Emerald Gem frowned, shaking her head. "You misunderstand.... Petal Shine has been like this for *hours*, and we can't figure out why."

Shining Armor tried to help Petal Shine up from the ground, but she pushed him away with her hooves as she giggled. "When did it start?" he asked.

"She had been out collecting giant Funflowers for our float in the garden earlier...." Emerald explained. She pointed at the float, which displayed shapes of the sun and moon. "When we came back from having our lunch, she was here just like this."

"How peculiar." While Cadance couldn't determine the cause of the laughter, she knew what to do to help. "This should do the trick." She braced her hooves on the ground, summoned her magical energy, and pointed her horn at Petal Shine. A swirl of blue aura floated to the pony. Within seconds, the giggles subsided.

Petal Shine stood up, confused. She looked up at the starry sky. "It's nighttime? Did I fall asleep?"

"What's the last thing you remember?" Emerald Gem asked.

"I was smelling a giant Funflower to make sure it would go nicely with the other flowers on our float, and then I guess I fell asleep."

Cadance, Shining Armor, and Emerald all exchanged worried looks. Funflower allergies were fairly common (Even Twilight Sparkle's friend Big McIntosh had one), so perhaps the pony had simply been allergic. But a voice deep down told Cadance that there was something more to this flowery incident.

And she was going to get to the root of it.

CHAPTER

8

Caught off Royal Guard

The Royal Guard hopefuls galloped back and forth, pounding their strong hooves into the dirt and grass. The field was a constellation of divots. Shining Armor stood at the helm, wearing his Royal Guard commander's uniform with pride. He barked out orders as part of a training exercise meant to prepare the stallions for anything and everything. If the ponies didn't react correctly to the order given, they were "out." The exercise would continue until one stallion stood victorious.

"Right flank...MARCH!"

The stallions turned right, all except for one with a dusty-orange mane, who spun left. "Topaz, out!" called Shining Armor. The pony hung his head and trotted to the sideline to meet the others who had met a similar fate. Now there were only four ponies left in the exercise.

"About-TURN!"

Three of the stallions turned in a circle to the left instead of right as they were supposed to. Shining Armor pointed his hoof at the one pony who had performed the move correctly. He was a strong, towering golden stallion. Everypony knew he was the best, most dedicated potential soldier of the bunch. Practically a horseshoe-in. "Jasper Hoof wins the drill-off!" He stood at attention and didn't even crack a smile.

Princess Cadance had been secretly watching the tryouts from the stands, hoping to show a little support for Shining Armor without getting in his way. She hadn't planned on revealing herself to the stallions, but it seemed like the perfect time to give the fellows a break.

"Darling!" Princess Cadance shouted. "How about giving the boys a breather?"

"Cady, what are you doing here?" he said through his teeth. He widened his eyes. "We've got a lot to do today...."

"Oh, come on, Mr. Serious," Cadance teased. She mimicked his tight-lipped facial expression. "You and the stallions still need to eat lunch, right? I'll have the kitchen bring down a picnic so they can check out the garden."

Over his shoulder, the princess saw the ponies' ears perk up. Even Jasper Hoof, who was all business, seemed hopeful. Shining Armor glanced back at them. "I guess they have been working really hard...." He smiled as he caved. "How do you manage to convince me of everything you want?"

The princess batted her eyelashes, innocent as ever. "I don't know...magic?"

"I'm under your spell, my dear." Shining Armor turned back to his stallions and yelled, "Let's move out, recruits! LUNCH!"

Ponies from all over the Empire were already frolicking in the revamped garden, even though the celebration was officially still a few days away. They appeared to be nothing short of entranced by the new-found natural beauty of the castle grounds. And for good reason—the flower selections were like nothing Cadance had ever seen before. The blooms were every color of the rainbow and ranged from the size of a new-born foal to a full-grown stallion!

Some of the plant varieties were unique; Cadance thought they must grow only in the Crystal Empire. She wanted to ask the names of them, but there was no sign of Olivine Jewel and her two friends. *Hmmm,* thought the princess. *They must finally be fin-ished.* She made a mental note to commend them on their excellent contributions.

Cadance was filled with pride as she strolled through the garden and watched the ponies have fun. Some Crystal ponies lay in the grass, staring up at the clouds. Others laughed and some hummed upbeat tunes. A few sat mesmerized as they stared into the shimmering water of the centerpiece fountain of "Spike the Brave and Glorious." The statue dragon had real emeralds for eyes and squirted water out of its mouth, a reminder of the fire Spike had lit in honor of the Equestria Games.

The Royal Guard hopefuls had no trouble finding a nice patch of grass to enjoy their picnic of sandwiches, made from Granny Smith's own stock of zap apple jam, shipped all the way from Sweet Apple Acres. Shining Armor laughed heartily at somepony's joke, then stopped himself and nodded, serious. He was doing his best to retain some sense of authority while still being one of the stallions. It was endearing.

A bright-orange monarch butterfly landed on Cadance's muzzle for a moment and took off toward the fountain. Cadance watched its journey as it landed on the nose of a pony she recognized as Glitter Mint. The filly didn't react to the butterfly. She just kept staring intensely at something in the water.

Cadance trotted over, intrigued by the odd behavior. "What are you looking at, Glitter Mint?"

"Myself," the filly answered dreamily. "I'm *so* fascinating...."

"I am, too.... Look at me...." mused the pony next to her. She was doing the exact same thing as Glitter Mint. "I can't stop looking at my face. It's like I've never seen it before." Her eyes bore into her watery reflection. She wasn't even blinking!

Nearby, a pair of ponies were humming so loud they sounded like a hive of bees. It wasn't a melody—just noise. The ponies had the same glazed-over look as Glitter Mint and her friend. They appeared to be having a "conversation," but they were just humming back and forth to each other.

What?! Cadance suddenly felt as if she'd entered an alternate reality. Maybe she had! She rubbed her eyes and tried to will herself out of the vision. But when the princess opened them, everything was the same as before. It was real.

Olivine, Fire Opal, and Star Seed hid in one of the Humzinnia bushes nearby. The three little ponies had clothespins on their muzzles to make sure they didn't accidentally sniff the flowers themselves. They watched the scene unfold with equal parts fascination and shock.

"I can't believe the enchanted flowers actually worked!" Olivine smiled in wonder. "My grandpa Alabaster always told me stories of magic plants, but I thought he was making most of it up. Especially the part about how fast they grow."

"It's actually kind of awesome," marveled Fire Opal. Her voice sounded nasal because of the clothespin. "Nice job, Olivine."

Olivine beamed.

"You're *sure* nopony will be harmed?" Star Seed asked again. "It's just, like, a weird way to connect with nature?"

"Of course! They're totally fine," Olive assured them. She watched as a teal Unicorn sniffed a gigantic white Lazilily and lay down on the grass, yawning. "The effects wear off eventually." But Princess Cadance didn't know that, Olivine thought. Maybe she would regret making a bunch of ponies do all the work.

CHAPTER

9

Panic! at the Castle

Back at the castle, word had already spread that there was some sort of funny business at the garden. When Cadance and Shining Armor burst through the double doors, their best staff members were already researching possible causes for the commotion. The ponies were gathered around a table covered with a hundred books pulled from the Crystal Empire Library.

"Any ideas?" Princess Cadance looked to the group, feeling panicked. "I've never seen anything this... *bizarre*."

"It's definitely Discord!" Shimmer Berry shouted, pointing to a picture of the draconequus in an old tome entitled *The Chaotic Age of Equestria*. "Has all his trademarks! Silly sights, silly sounds, silly smells..."

"The changelings are here!" cried Lieutenant Jade Wing as he flipped through a book on Queen Chrysalis. "And they're impersonating our friends. Don't changelings hum? I think I read that in here somewhere...."

"King Sombra is back," whispered the butler pony, frightened. "He's going to suck all the love out of the Empire again...."

"Whatever it is, we need a solution." Shining Armor furrowed his brow in frustration. "Fast." He was particularly annoyed because his entire team of recruits was now acting strange, too. The nimble stallions had suddenly become clumsy and uncoordinated. Jasper Hoof had tripped over his horseshoes when Shining Armor had called the ponies to stand at attention.

"I don't think it's a plot by an evil force," Cadance thought aloud. "It's more harmless than that...." She paced back and forth. "It seems like the work of an individual."

"That doesn't make sense. What sort of grumpy pony would want to sabotage the Garden Hearts Celebration?" wondered Shimmer Berry.

Suddenly, an image of Olivine Jewel frowning at the back of the school group flashed in Cadance's mind. "Perhaps it was somepony who wanted to stand out...."

"What do you mean?" A puzzled Shining Armor cocked his head to the side. "You know who did this, Cady?"

"I think I do," Princess Cadance said, nodding. "It's all my fault. I'm going to find her and set everything straight." Before anypony could protest, the princess was galloping out the door in a flash of pink and gold.

CHAPTER

10

The Crystal Crown Café

"Olivine Jewel!" Princess Cadance called out over the cacophony of hums, giggles, and snores of the enchanted ponies in the garden. "Are you there, Olivine? I need to talk to you!" She trotted through the hedge maze and past the row of beautiful topiaries cut into the shapes of animals and hearts. The sight reminded her of the vision—the whole reason why Cadance had pushed this plan into action.

"It's gotten worse." Cadance hung her head as she approached a pair of ponies giggling uncontrollably, just as Petal Shine had. Cadance summoned her magic and directed it at them. But, unfortunately, the spell the ponies were under was too strong, and the wild fits of laughter continued.

"Oh, Celestia, what have I done?" Princess Cadance sighed. She kept walking, halfheartedly looking for the little green filly.

The problem with glimpses of the future, she thought, was that they were incomplete pictures. How was the princess to know that behind the sound of pony laughter she'd heard was some sort of spell forcing them to giggle at everything? Cadance now realized she had been twisting the vision to suit her own desires. It was about as helpful as trying to decipher a pattern of leaves in the bottom of her teacup.

Cadance took a sip of the piping-hot dandelion tea. "Thank you for the tea, Lilac Quartz, but I really can't stay." The princess had come to the café only to look for Olivine, but she'd been ushered to the best table.

"Your Majesty, I insist!" the motherly mare fussed. She carried over a platter of warm Crystal berry tarts and placed them gingerly on the table. "At least have a tart before you go."

Cadance shoved a tart into her mouth and spoke through the crumbly sweetness. "Have you seen your daughter? It's urgent that I find her...."

"I have just one more treat for you, Princess!" Lilac Quartz trotted to the kitchen in the back, ignoring the question.

"What's that Olivine done now?" a mare whispered, leaning in from the next table. Cadance recognized her as Sweet Leaf from the day of the Heartsong. "Poor Lilac Quartz can't even rein her filly in...."

Across from her, another mare from their group that day—Rose Water—shook her head. "That little pony is up to something bad."

"What do you mean?" Cadance asked, growing impatient. The sooner she found Olivine, the sooner she would solve the mystery in the garden. The princess knew she was on the right track. Olivine had been down in the area the entire time. She must have seen—or done— something.

"She's just always running off and disappearing, doing Celestia knows what." Rose Water raised her brow in judgment. Her bushy pink mane bounced as she shook her head. "*My* daughter, Fire Opal, would never act in that manner. . . ."

"Neither would my sweet little Star Seed." Sweet Leaf nodded. "She's a model student."

These two gossips weren't Princess Cadance's cup of tea at all.

"Excuse me, ladies." Princess Cadance stood up. "I'm actually here to speak with Lilac Quartz about a special honor that Olivine Jewel is going to be given by the castle." The two mares' jaws dropped. "Good day."

CHAPTER
11

Master Gardener Alabaster Stone

Even though the princess had sent word to the castle that she might be gone for a few hours, Cadance didn't think her investigation would lead her all the way to the outskirts of the Crystal Empire. But here she was, behind Lilac Quartz, stomping through the wild foliage to an old cottage.

"Olivine Jewel comes here all the time to

visit her grandfather Alabaster Stone," Lilac Quartz explained. "She's quite attached to him. Loves his old stories about the Crystal Empire before King Sombra." Lilac made a sad face. "When he can remember them, that is…"

"It's so isolated out here," Cadance observed. "Why doesn't he live closer to the center of the Crystal Empire?"

Lilac Quartz motioned to all the over-grown plants in crystal pots on the porch. "He's got more room for his plants out here." She smiled. "He doesn't grow half as much as he used to, but he's still got that same gardener spirit that he had all those years ago when he worked at the castle." The mare twisted the knob and shoved open the heavy wooden door. "But I'm sure Olivine told you all about that."

"No, she didn't mention it...." Princess Cadance narrowed her eyes. "Alabaster worked in the castle garden?"

"Oh yeah! He was the greatest pony in all of Equestria at what he did," Lilac Quartz replied, waxing nostalgic. "They even did an interview with him in the Equestrian Botanical Society journal—"Flora and Foalna"—about the southern plants he was able to grow in the Crystal climate!"

As Cadance followed Lilac inside, she immediately saw evidence of the stallion's long and illustrious career. The warm cottage was packed with plants and memorabilia. Her eyes landed on a framed photo. The image was yellowed from age but clear—it was a young Alabaster standing proudly next to a familiar sign that read, EMPIRE GARDEN, BY MASTER GARDENER "A. S."

"So *he's* the famous master gardener! Wow." Cadance brightened. "'A.S.' stands for 'Alabaster Stone.'"

"Who's askin'?" grumbled the old stallion, waking up from a nap in his cozy chair. "I didn't do it." He coughed. "What?"

"Hi, Dad!" Lilac trotted over, setting down the basket of Crystal Crown Café goodies she'd brought over for him. "This is Her Majesty, Princess Cadance!"

Cadance gave a friendly bow. Alabaster frowned. "Princess, huh?"

"Olive didn't tell you she was helping to fix the castle gardens for the big Garden Hearts Celebration?"

"No," answered Alabaster Stone. "But she shouldn't be. Those royals—"

"Be nice, please?" Lilac interrupted

through gritted teeth. "We're looking for Olivine. Have you seen her today?"

"It could have been today…coulda been a week ago." He scratched his thin white mane with his hoof. The stallion stood up slowly and began to shuffle toward the kitchen. "She was here with a couple little fillies. But I was havin' my nap, so I didn't get up." Alabaster pointed to his bookshelf. "They were nosin' through my stuff, though."

"Did Olivine or the other ponies happen to take anything?" asked Princess Cadance, scanning the cluttered room. It would probably be hard to notice anything missing. Perhaps they'd borrowed some gardening tools. There were certainly plenty to choose from here.

"How should I know?" Alabaster grunted. "Look at this place!" He began to fix himself a bowl of oats. "At least the only thing I have of value is safe. Right there on the brown table in the corner."

Lilac Quartz trotted over to the table in question. There was nothing on it but dust and a clean square space. "Are you sure, Dad? Your enchanted seed box…well, it's gone."

"What?" Alabaster shuffled his hooves as fast as he could. "But…but…it's dangerous." The color drained from his face. "Daffospills…and Reflection Roses…? Giggling Funflowers, Humzinnias, *and* Lazililies? If anypony plants those seeds and smells those flowers, we're going to have a major problem on our hooves."

Princess Cadance thought of the ponies

trapped in the garden. "I think we already do." She gulped. "Mr. Stone, can you help us fix it?"

"I—I…would, but I…" the old pony stammered, hoof to his head, "…can't remember how."

CHAPTER

12

Crystal-Blue Persuasion

On their frantic trip back to the castle, the trio passed by the Crystal Heart. Much to the princess's dismay, the light was now at a constant flicker. In her own heart, Cadance knew that the malfunction was happening because of all the citizens who were under the spell of the magical flowers. How could a pony embody true light and love when they were in an altered state of mind? It was impossible. Cadance couldn't believe the mess she'd made of everything.

"Hurry! It's not far!" Princess Cadance called over her shoulder. "Mr. Stone, I just know that if you step hoof in the garden, it'll help you remember something." She forged ahead across the grassy field with Alabaster and Lilac Quartz in tow. The old stallion hadn't stopped complaining the whole time.

"The castle doesn't deserve my help," Alabaster muttered to his daughter. "They didn't want me back after King Sombra was defeated!"

"Nonsense, Dad." Lilac Quartz frowned. "*You* told them it would be too much work to fix the garden again."

"Hogwash!" Alabaster replied, raising a

bushy eyebrow. "That's not how I remember it. . . ."

"My point exactly," Lilac Quartz teased, then tried an alternate approach. She batted her big, aqua-colored eyes at him. "Just try to help out for Olivine, okay?"

A loud noise began to drown out their conversation as the three ponies arrived at the garden gates. In Princess Cadance's absence, the problem had multiplied tenfold. There were now hundreds of ponies trotting around the area in various states of enchantment.

Unicorns, Pegasi, and Earth ponies of all ages hummed and giggled, lounged and stared at themselves in the fountain. The swaths of ribbons and lights, along with the brilliant colors of the flowers, gave the whole scene a false sense of festivity. But this

Armor. Maybe he and his Royal Guard are on their way!"

"Oh, uh…Princess?" Lilac Quartz bit her lip and pointed straight ahead. "I think that ship has sailed, dear." Sure enough, Shining Armor was there, surrounded by his guards. There was no rescue mission under way. Instead, the uniformed, burly stallions were giggling like a Filly Scout troop at a slumber party.

"Shining Armor!" Cadance cried out in anguish. "Don't worry, boys! I'll save you!" Cadance calmly began to rack her brains for spells that might help, but was coming up short. If only she could recall the vision and look closer. She had to be missing something. . . .

"I have an idea," Cadance announced,

springing to action. "I'll be right back." She took off into the air.

Just outside the garden, in the exact spot her vision had depicted, the princess made one last attempt. Cadance closed her eyes, painting the picture in her mind. Everything melted away, and there she was again in the dream state: the lush green grass and the sun shining on her pink face, the fresh air, and the heavy scent of flower blossoms. In the distance, intricate topiaries lined the horizon. Hundreds of ponies were singing. *Hundreds of ponies were singing!*

"That's it!" Cadance shouted as she snapped out of her vision. She could almost hear Princess Luna's voice in her head reciting the old sorcery adage: *When the spell is strong and has been far prolonged, a familiar song may right the wrong.* It was worth a try.

The pink Alicorn took off, spreading her purple-tipped wings and soaring back to the heart of the commotion. She floated above the garden and focused her energy. A soft blue haze of magical aura from her horn surrounded her neck to amplify her voice.

Then the princess began to sing with all her heart.

"When the Crystal snow is no longer chilly, join voices with every colt and every filly!" At this, two or three ponies craned their necks and looked up at her.

Cadance's pulse quickened with excitement. It was working! She kept singing. *"There's only one solution, and we've made a resolution...."* Her pretty voice rang out, awakening even more confused ponies. Some of them began to join in. The sound grew stronger and richer with each note.

"We'll lift our spirits to the sky. Our hearts grow full and our hooves rise up high." The rest of the spellbound citizens snapped back to reality like kernels of popcorn on a warm hearth. More and more ponies joined in the song. *"Hooves cold, hearts warm; cold hooves, warm hearts! Garden Hearts, we all take paaaaaart!"*

A searing flash of blue light washed over everything as Cadance felt her body plummeting to the ground. The Crystal Heart had been powered.

CHAPTER

13

The Horse Awakens

The sound of birds was the first thing Cadance noticed. No humming, no incessant laughter—just the sweet song and twittering of the blue jays. And whispers. She blinked and rubbed away the remnants of the bright light. Cadance opened her eyes to a crowd of curious ponies standing around, scratching their heads, and trying to piece together what exactly had happened.

"Why are we in the garden?" wondered Jasper Hoof, looking around.

"Did I fall asleep?" asked Glitter Mint, rubbing her eyes.

"Is the princess okay?" Gemma called out, standing on her tippy-hooves to see.

"Cady!" Shining Armor rushed over to his wife, breaking through the mob of Crystal ponies. He helped her up from the ground. "You did it! You saved everypony! I don't know how...but one minute I was leading my stallions to practice, and the next I was singing "Cold Hooves, Warm Hearts" with you flying above us." He gestured to the crowd. "I have a feeling there was a lot more between that..."

"You have no idea," Cadance sighed, breaking a tiny smile. What a relief! Her citizens were freed from the spell, and nopony was hurt. Her eyes scanned the crowd and landed on a particular young green filly who was hunched over in the dirt. Her pink mane hung down over her eyes, and she was sniffling.

"Olive!" Lilac Quartz reprimanded, approaching her daughter. "Why in Equestria would you steal Grandpa's seeds?" The mother's face was flush with embarrassment. "You nearly caused the entire Crystal Empire to be trapped in their enchantments forever!"

"I know," Olive said, and sniffed. "I'm so sorry, Mama. I didn't think it would end up like this...." Olive stood up and shrugged. "All I wanted was a little bit of revenge."

"Revenge?" Princess Cadance asked as she walked toward them. "I don't understand.... Who has wronged you, Olivine Jewel?"

"At first I was annoyed at *you*, Princess Cadance...." Olivine admitted.

Everypony gasped.

Cadance slumped down. "But why?"

Olive's face twisted into a frown. "All this time after the Crystal Empire returned and you've never even offered Grandpa his job back!" Olivine paced, motioning with her hooves. "And then you force *me* of all ponies to fix his garden?"

"I didn't even know—"

"But everypony else loved doing the castle's dirty work. They were having so much fun digging and planting seeds! And, as usual, I was alone in a corner." Olivine pointed to Star Seed and Fire Opal. "I just wanted to be more like them. I wanted them to like *me*... and I realized I had the perfect way to impress everypony."

"My magic seed collection?" Grandpa Alabaster coughed. "You know better than that, Little 'Vine." Olive looked down at her hooves in shame.

"You didn't need to do that to impress us," Star Seed laughed. "All you had to do was, like, chill out."

"Seriously," Fire Opal agreed, flipping her rainbow mane. "We liked you before, and we won't stop now."

Olivine's eyes grew huge. "Really?"

"Of course!" Star Seed and Fire Opal embraced their new friend in a hug.

Olivine turned to Princess Cadance. "I can't believe I made so many huge mistakes and misjudgments. I'm so sorry, Princess."

The filly took a deep breath. "I understand if you want to ban me from the Crystal Empire—"

"What?" Princess Cadance interrupted. She couldn't help but chuckle. "Oh, Olivine Jewel . . . *I'm* the one who should be apologizing to you. I saw that something was bothering you at the Hearts and Hooves Day Heartsong, and I didn't even bother to dig deeper. I should have asked what the root of the problem was, instead of assuming I could solve it." Princess Cadance put her hoof on Olive's shoulder. "I feel that this mess has been both of our doing. So what do you say to getting the garden ready for the big celebration tomorrow"—Cadance extended her pink hoof—"*together?*"

"I would love that," Olivine laughed with relief. She hoof-bumped Cadance. "The funny thing is…through all of this, I found out that I actually really enjoy gardening. A lot."

Lilac Quartz rolled her eyes. "I've been telling you that for years!"

"Me too!" Grandpa Alabaster grunted with a satisfied smirk. "Always had the talent."

"What can I say?" Olivine smiled and shrugged. "Sometimes a filly has got to sow her own oats to figure it out, even if the seeds were planted early on."

Olivine trotted over to a bush covered in brilliant red roses. She plucked one and presented it to Princess Cadance. "I grew this one by myself. No magic spells." She smiled wide with pride.

Cadance held the bloom to her muzzle and inhaled. The sweet scent was fresh and pure. "It's perfect."

"And so is your cutie mark!" Fire Opal pointed at the pony's flank. Sure enough, resting upon Olivine Jewel's flank was a beautiful cutie mark of a green heart-shaped jewel. It looked almost like the Crystal Heart itself, but it had swirly, curly green vines growing around it. "It looks almost like ... *a Garden Heart*."

CHAPTER
14

garden Hearts Celebration

Flower petals fell from the sky in a rainbow of colors. They fluttered onto the ponies, sticking to their manes and covering the shimmering crystal ground in a soft, fragrant carpet. Olivine Jewel could hardly believe that she was sitting on the royal floral float with baby Flurry Heart, right between Princess Cadance and Prince

Shining Armor, as Grand Mareshall of the Garden Hearts Celebration parade. The Crystal Heart shone brightly on a platform below them, surrounded by hundreds of blue and white flowers. It felt like a dream.

"Princess Cadance?" Olivine asked, throwing a hoof-ful of fresh petals onto the crowd below. She could see her mother, Lilac Quartz, standing next to a very grumpy Sweet Leaf and Rose Water.

"Happy Spring, mares and gentlecolts!" Princess Cadance waved her hoof at the ponies. "Yes, Olive?"

"Why did you choose me to be Grand Mareshall? After everything I did?"

Princess Cadance laughed. "You're the pony who reminds me of spring."

"I am?" Olivine scrunched up her muzzle. "Why?"

"Because no matter how cold the winter—or how big our mistakes—may be, there is always time to start fresh again." Cadance grinned and gave Olive a nudge. "Don't you agree?" For the first time ever, Olivine did. Her Crystal heart had finally bloomed, right along with the flowers. And after watching Olivine grow, Cadance was brimming with light and love.

Don't Miss

Princess Celestia
and The Summer of Royal Waves

by G. M. Berrow

Don't Miss

Keep reading for a special surprise from Princess Cadance

Dear reader,

I created these bonus pages just for you while Flurry Heart was down for her nap! Enjoy the activities and share them with your friends.

Love,

Princess Cadance

An A-Maze-ing Garden

The ponies of Crystal Prep have been working so hard to help Princess Cadance fix up the Crystal Empire Gardens. Along with planting beautiful flowers, they have decided to design a hedge maze! Can you help Princess Cadance find her way through the hedges back to the castle?

Colors of Your Crystal Heart

Princess Cadance has a dilemma! The shimmering Crystal Heart is looking a little bit dull today. It should be filled with rainbow colors and sparkling light. Can you help the love shine through by coloring in the heart?

♥On Guard!

Shining Armor takes great pride in training his
Royal Guard stallions to be the very best in Equestria.
They play all sorts of games and do exercises to make
sure that they are strong and ready for *anything*.
Shining Armor loves each soldier's individuality, but
when they are a team they must look uniform.
Can you help Shining Armor get his guards in
line by circling the differences below?

example

Spread the Love

The Crystal Empire is powered by the magical Crystal Heart, which runs on the love and positive feelings of the ponies. In addition to events like the Heartsong, everypony likes to compliment one another. It makes them feel wonderful! Use the space below to write some compliments about the friends and family members in your life. Then let them know how you feel to spread light and love like a Crystal Pony!

Name: _____

Compliment: _____

_____

Name: _____

Compliment: _____

_____

Name: _____

Compliment: _____

_____

A garden of Friends

Strong friendships can take time to grow. Sometimes
you have to plant the seeds of friendship and help them
along with silly jokes and fun times together! Think
about a friend and write about them here.
What makes this friend so special to you?
How have you grown with them?

_____

_____

_____

_____

_____

_____

_____

_____

_____

_____

_____

_____

_____

Heartsongs and Sing-alongs

The Hearts & Hooves Day Heartsong is only one of the many traditions the Crystal Ponies uphold in their land. At this event, the ponies join together in song to show their love for one another and for their beautiful home. What is your favorite song to sing? Choose one that makes you feel happy, and write the lyrics here!

NaME OF SONG: _____

ARTIST: _____

I LIKE THIS SONG BECAUSE: _____

_____

_____

_____

LYRICS: _____

_____

_____

_____

_____

_____

_____

A Grand Time Together

In the story, the young pony Olivine Jewel has a special relationship with her grandpa Alabaster Stone. She loves listening to everything he know about plants and gardening, as well as just visiting with him over a cup of hot cocoa. Do you have a grandparent or an adult in your life that you like to spend time with? If so, what is your favorite activity to do with them? What's the most interesting fact they've told you? Write about them below.

_____

_____

_____

_____

_____

_____

_____

_____

_____

_____

Digging for Words

The Crystal Ponies were so busy digging in the garden that they didn't realize they covered up these words with dirt! Can you help the ponies unearth the words below? Circle each one. *Hint:* They can be found running forward, backward, up, down, and diagonally!

CADANCE

CRYSTAL ✓

FLOWER ✓

GARDEN

HEARTSONG

LOVE ✓

OLIVINE ·

H P K E K E F E T K A N
A R E W O L F Y L P O D
A I V R M M C G S R J I
G N O S T R A E H N E C
I C L Y N O C S S E Y E
Q E R S A N E L W I E I
L S R Y A G A R D E N M
L S C D S K U D H O T M
R A A I G T H E G N N C
E C K F S C A N R E G S
P P E N I V I L O D C E

Floating on Flowers

Princess Cadance has a wonderful idea to include a parade in her spring celebration. All the ponies are invited to create floats covered entirely in fresh flowers. If you were designing a float for Cadance's parade, what would it look like? Draw it below. Don't forget to include lots of colorful flowers!

A Rose by Any Other Name

Shining Armor loves to tease his wife by calling her "Mi Amore Cadenza," which is really her full name! But the princess prefers her nickname, "Cadance." Can you connect the names of the ponies below with their nicknames?

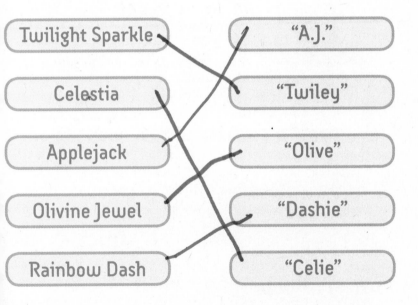

Twilight Sparkle	"A.J."
Celestia	"Twiley"
Applejack	"Olive"
Olivine Jewel	"Dashie"
Rainbow Dash	"Celie"

grow Your garden

Spring is a glorious season! After the long, cold winter, the sun comes out and plants begin to grow again. Have you ever tried to grow anything? Have an adult help you plant some seeds and use the space below to record their progress. You can plant flowers, vegetables, or even herbs for cooking!

Name of Plant:

_____

Draw a Picture of the Seed Here:

Date Planted: _____

This Plant Should Be
Watered every: _____

PROGRESS

Week 1: _____
_____
_____

Week 2: _____
_____
_____

Week 3: _____
_____
_____

DRaW a PictuRe of youR PLaNt HeRe: